For Tanja, Monika and Luka
and in memory of a proud grandfather Branko Sunajko

GOOD KNIGHT, SLEEP TIGHT
by David Melling

British Library Cataloguing in Publication Data
A catalogue record of this book is available from
the British Library.
ISBN 0 340 86092 8 (HB)

Copyright © David Melling 2005

The right of David Melling to be identified as
the author and illustrator of this Work has been asserted
by him in accordance with the Copyright, Designs and
Patents Act 1988.

First edition published 2005
10 9 8 7 6 5 4 3 2 1

Published by Hodder Children's Books
a division of Hodder Headline Limited
338 Euston Road London NW1 3BH

Printed in China

GOOD KNIGHT
SLEEP TIGHT

written and illustrated by

DAVID MELLING

Hodder
Children's
Books

A division of Hodder Headline Limited

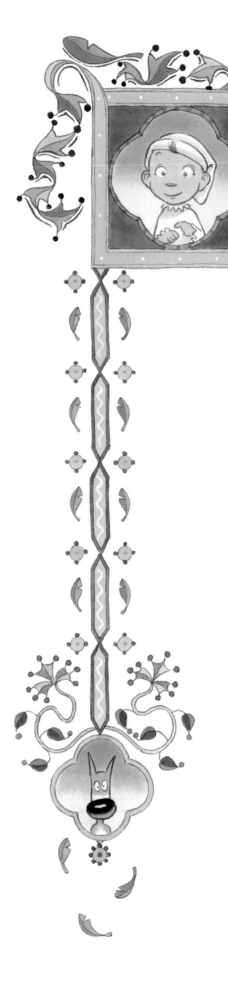

A NEW SOUND
echoed along the
corridors of the castle.
To the king and queen
was born a
royal princess.

The prince
had a baby sister.

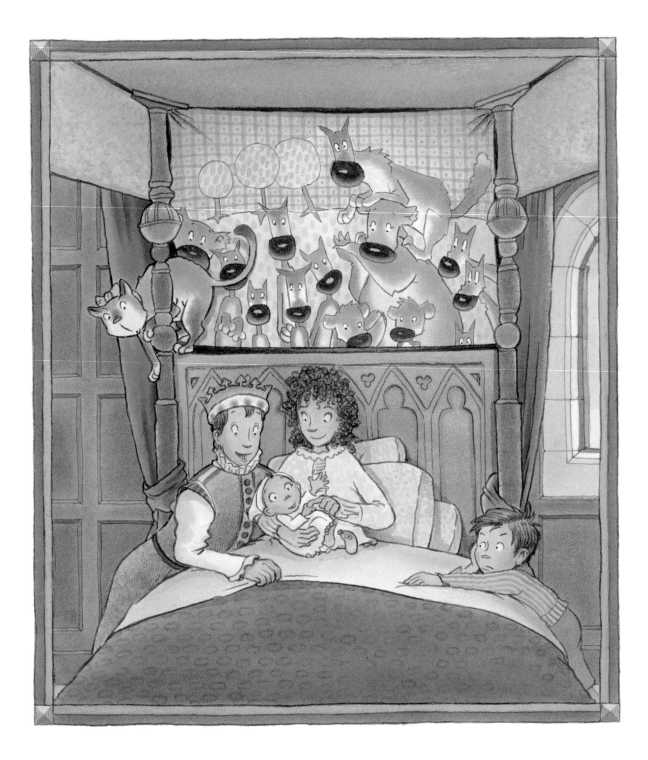

He couldn't see what all the fuss was about.

Among the many
    splendid presents was
        the softest, fluffiest pillow
            in the kingdom.

But one day
    the fat royal cat
    squashed it flat!

The poor princess cried.

And cried.

And cried.

So the king popped over for a little chat with his loyal knight.

'Fill this with something soft and fluffy!' he barked.

'And hurry!'

The knight leapt into action.

He was so quick there wasn't even enough time to finish the senter

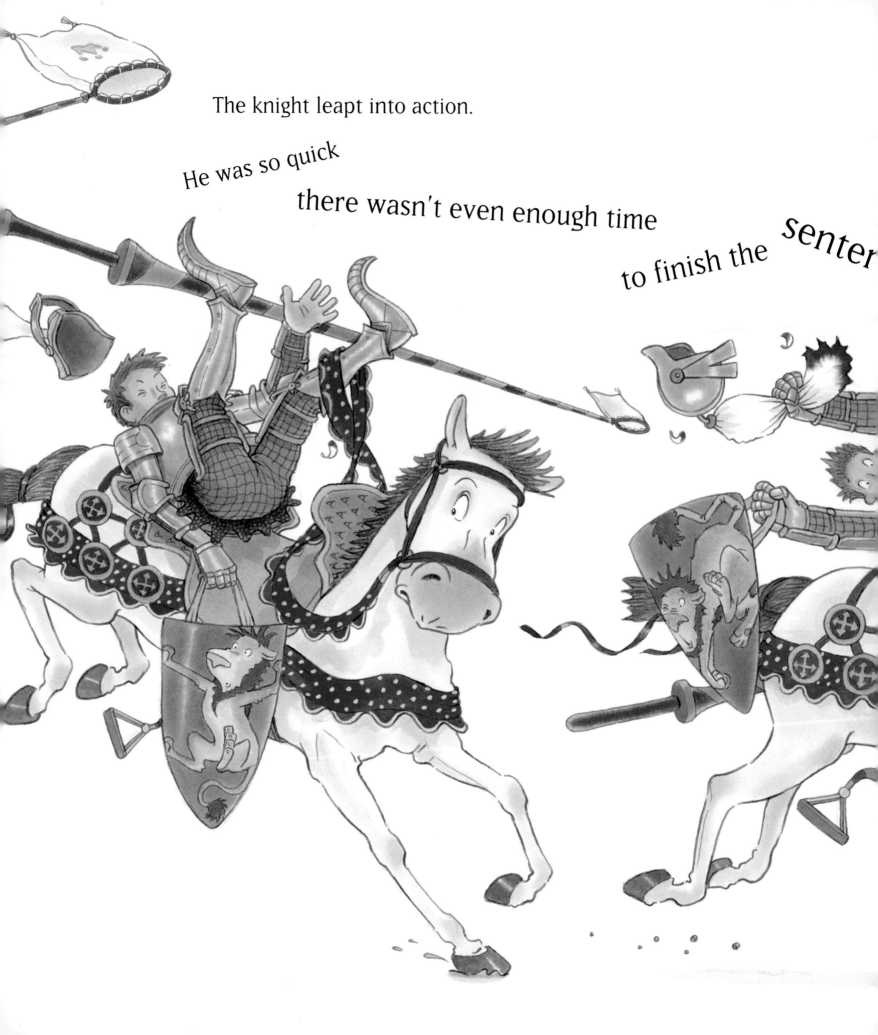

Deep inside the wild wood prickly bears rubbed their grumbly tummies. 'Lunch time!' they slurped.

But the knight was thinking about his quest. 'I wonder if I could borrow some bear hair to put in the royal pillow,' he thought, and decided to take a closer look.

Two minutes later the grizzled bears shuffled back into the shadows, rubbing their sore bottoms and mumbling to themselves.

'Well really, it's hardly fair. We just wanted a quick nibble. No need for that...'

Bear hair lay everywhere!

The knight filled the pillow and gave it to the horse.
'Is this pillow soft enough for the princess?' he asked.
'Neigh!' said the horse. (He thought it was too scratchy.)

Nobody noticed slinky shadows curling around the
tree trunks.

A jumble of wolves howwwled from the trees — they sniffed the knight, they sniffed the horse, then sniffed off.

Wolf hair lay everywhere!

The knight filled the pillow again and gave it to the horse.
'Is **this** pillow soft enough for the princess?' he asked.
'Neigh!' said the horse. (He thought it was too bristly.)

Just then...

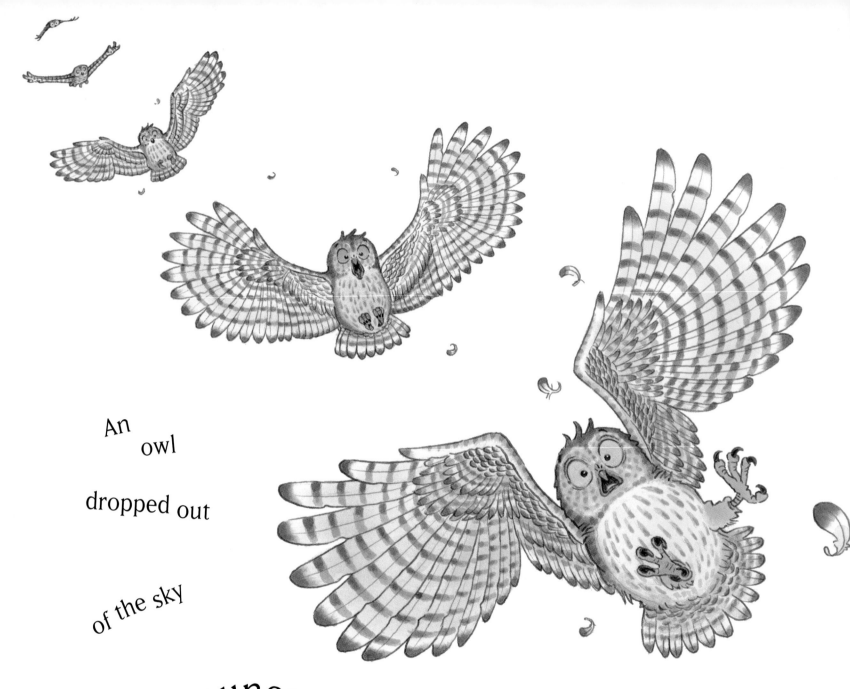

An owl

dropped out

of the sky

and bounced off the knight's head.

Feathers fluttered gently to the floor.

'That's it!' cried the knight.
'I'll make a pillow of feathers!'

'If it's feathers you want,'
said the dizzy owl, 'follow me.
I'll take you to see …

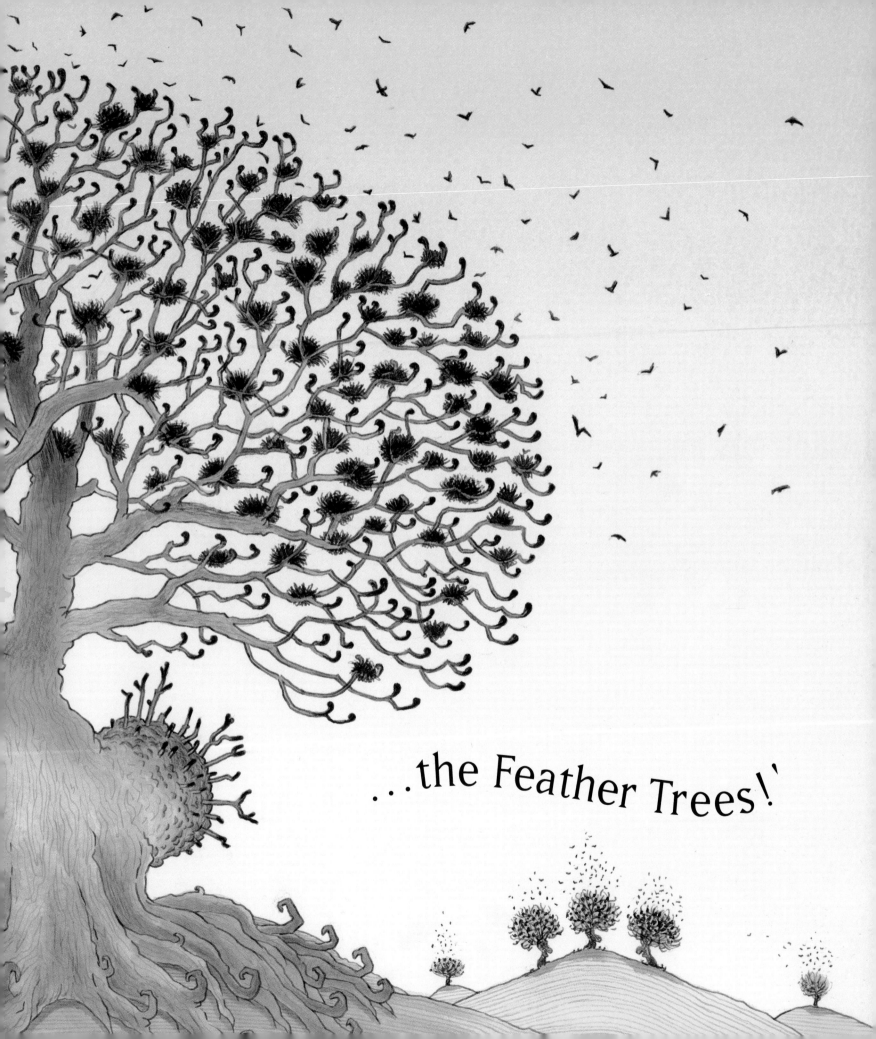

...the Feather Trees!'

So the knight and his 'I'm COMPLETELY scared of heights' horse clambered up into the branches.

All the birds gathered round to listen
to the knight's tale. There were feathers
everywhere!

When he had finished, the birds happily agreed
to help and plucked just enough feathers to fill
the pillow to the royal brim.

The knight and his faithful horse waved goodbye
and galloped and galloped and galloped until
they came back to the wild wood.

They wrestled and wriggled their way through its
darkest secrets…

…and $plopped$ out the other side.

No one in the castle had slept for a week so they were jolly pleased to see the knight return.

'Place that child upon that pillow before I go **bananas!**'

wailed the king.

Everyone held their breath …

The princess didn't!

So the prince leaned over and gave his baby sister a cuddle. The princess stopped crying. She smiled, blew a little bubble, and then went to sleep.

The king hugged the prince.

The queen hugged the prince.

At last the castle fell silent …

...except for the snoring that snuffled,

sleepily through the corridors.

Good knight, sleep tight.